KU-749-047

IN THE NIGHT KITCHEN

MAURICE SENDAK

PictureLions
An Imprint of HarperCollins*Publishers*

First published in Great Britain byThe Bodley Head 1971

First published in Picture Lions 1991. Picture Lions is an imprint of the Children's Division,
part of HarperCollins Publishers Limited,77-85 Fulham Palace Road, Hammersmith, London W6 8JB

Copyright © Maurice Sendak 1970

Printed and bound in Hong Kong

FOR SADIE AND PHILIP

DID YOU EVER HEAR OF MICKEY, HOW HE HEARD A RACKET IN THE NIGHT

AND FELL THROUGH THE DARK, OUT OF HIS CLOTHES

INTO THE LIGHT OF THE NIGHT KITCHEN?

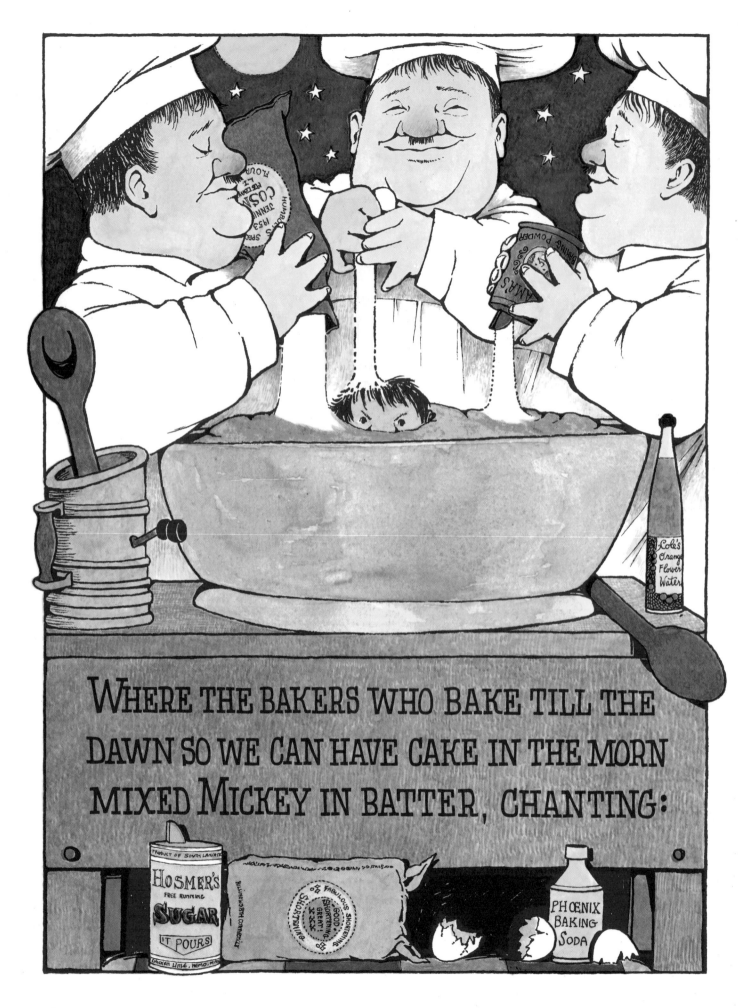

AND THEY PUT THAT BATTER UP TO BAKE

A DELICIOUS MICKEY-CAKE.

BUT RIGHT IN THE MIDDLE OF THE STEAMING AND THE MAKING AND THE SMELLING AND THE BAKING MICKEY POKED THROUGH AND SAID:

SO HE SKIPPED FROM THE OVEN & INTO BREAD DOUGH ALL READY TO RISE IN THE NIGHT KITCHEN.

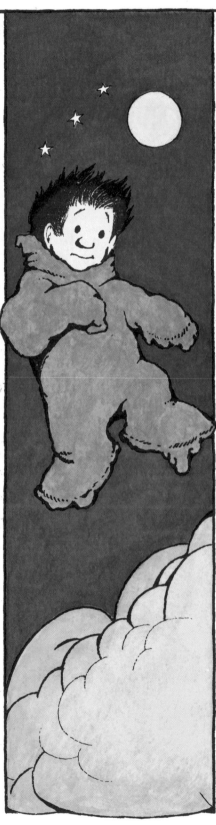

HE KNEADED AND PUNCHED IT
AND POUNDED AND PULLED

TILL IT LOOKED OKAY.

WHEN THE BAKERS RAN UP
WITH A MEASURING CUP, HOWLING:

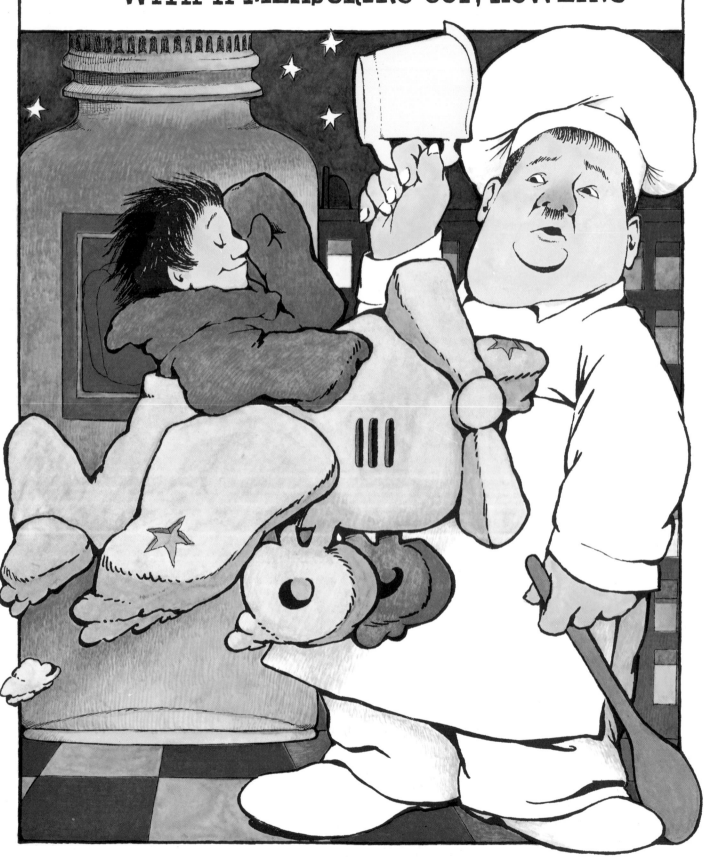

MICKEY THE MILKMAN DIVED DOWN TO THE BOTTOM

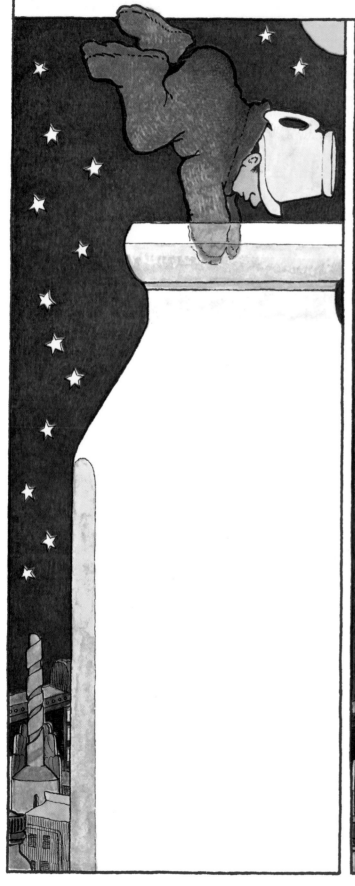

SO THE BAKERS THEY MIXED IT
AND BEAT IT AND BAKED IT.

MILK IN THE BATTER! MILK IN THE BATTER!
Mama's CREAM of TARTAR

COCK
·a·
DOODLE
DOO!

36

AND THAT'S WHY, THANKS TO MICKEY

WE HAVE CAKE EVERY MORNING